Love

BONNEY
PRESS

Published by Bonney Press,
an imprint of Hinkler Books Pty Ltd
45-55 Fairchild Street
Heatherton Victoria 3202 Australia
www.hinkler.com.au

BONNEY PRESS

© Hinkler Books Pty Ltd 2020

Author: Helen O'Dare
Illustrator: Nicola O'Byrne

ISBN: 978 1 4889 1927 5

Printed and bound in China

Love

Helen O'Dare

Nicola O'Byrne

This book is for all the special people in my life,
and especially for the most special of all, Reay and Bridie – HO'D

Love

can be **gigantic** like a **mountain,**
and **small** and **precious** like a **diamond.**

Love
stretches up, up, **tall** like a **tree**,
but secured by its **roots** so **deep**.

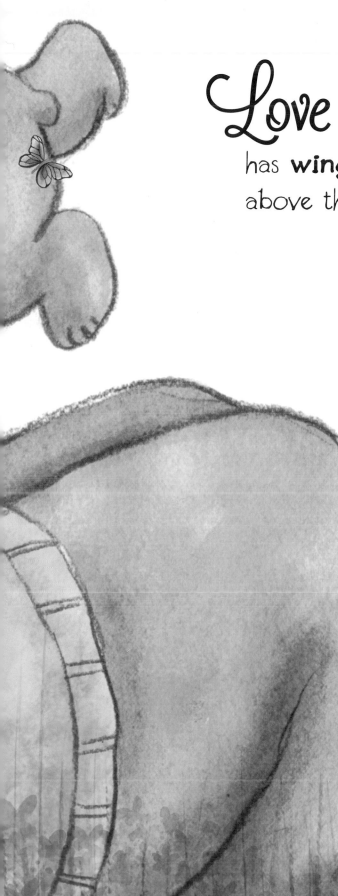

Love

has **wings** that help you **fly**
above the **clouds** in the **big blue sky**.

Love

is there in a **tickle** and a **giggle**
and an **enormous** belly-laugh **wiggle!**

Love

can be **loud** like a trumpet's **blares**
that sometimes **catch** you **unawares**!

Love

is a **book** and a **warm** milk mug,
and makes the **rainy** days all **snug.**

Love

can be **yummy,** like a **chocolate cake**
that we mixed and put in the **oven** to **bake.**

Love
can make you **sing** out **loud.**
You always make me feel so **proud!**

Love

can be **splashes** and **soap** and **bubbles**.
I will always **love** your **cuddles**!

*L*ove

is **strong** and **true** like a **big bear hug**
that you give to a **sleepy** little **snuggle-bug**.

Love
is **big** and **wide**
and **ocean deep**.
It's even **there**
when you're **asleep**.

Love
is all of these, it's true.
And that's how much **I love YOU!**